THE PICTURE

Story and pictures by

Catherine Brighton

faber and faber

LONDON · BOSTON

I am in bed.
I am hot.
I am ill.

Heavy eyes.
I watch the wall.
I watch the picture on the wall.

There is a girl in flowing clothes.
She moves.
She comes towards me.

She takes my hand.
I go.
I go into the picture.

It is cold.
She gives me a blanket.
We hurry through the snow.

She opens a door.
Her family are there.
The years roll back.

My heart is thudding.
I hear their laughter.
It is at a distance.

I am hot.
They bring me a drink.
It tastes of cloves.

We play.

It is silent.
Look.
I hold the baby.

It is time to go.
The snow.
The cold.
The door.

She takes my hand.

I am in bed.
I am better.
The picture is on the wall.
There is an extra blanket on my bed.